PUGLY
Bakes a Cake
PAMELA
BUTCHART
Illustrated by
GEMMA
CORRELL
nosy

Also by

Pamela Butchart:

Wigglesbottom Primary:

The Toilet Ghost

The Shark in the Pool

The Magic Hamster

Illustrated by Becka Moor

Baby Aliens Got My Teacher!

The Spy Who Loved School Dinners

My Head Teacher is a Vampire Rat!

Attack of the Demon Dinner Ladies

Illustrated by Thomas Flintham

For all the pugs I met at the Dundee Pug Party:

Rosco (hates TV)
Bow Bow (snorts)
Dolly (purrs like a cat)
Rudy & Daphne (steal babies' dummies)
Willow (can't turn around)
Bobo & Lulu (like to cuddle)
Frank (hates horses & Darth Vader)
Ralph (ear-licker)
Harley (one-eyed hunk)
Briegha (food thief)
Winston (LOVES cheese!)
Dolly (The Pugshu)
Manny (wees on people)
Django (hand-licker)
Precious (The Pugfather)

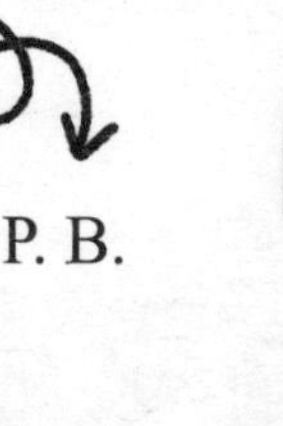

P. B.

First published in the UK in 2016 by Nosy Crow Ltd
The Crow's Nest, 10a Lant Street
London, SE1 1QR, UK

Nosy Crow and associated logos are trademarks and/or registered
trademarks of Nosy Crow Ltd

3 5 7 9 10 8 6 4 2

A CIP catalogue record for this book will be available from the British Library.

Printed and bound in the UK by Clays Ltd, St. Ives Plc

Papers used by Nosy Crow are made from wood grown in
sustainable forests.

ISBN: 978 0 85763 599 0

www.nosycrow.com

Chapter 1

Tobias Roberto Mozzarella Pugly!

OK, so that's not my REAL name. My real name is Pugly. But I'm never going to get on in life unless I THINK BIG. And you have to admit that Tobias Roberto Mozzarella Pugly is a

BIG NAME.

Pugly is a dog's name. And I'm MUCH more than just a dog. I'm a pug with

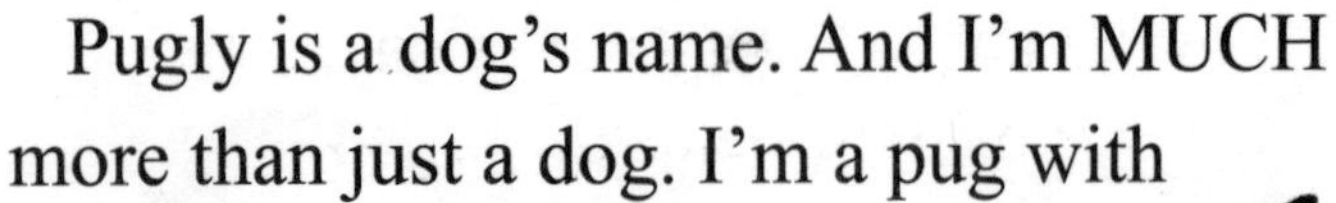

Clem the cat says that my ideas are RIDICULOUS. But they're not. She's probably just too SLEEPY to notice how good my ideas are because she's a cat and she sleeps ALLLLLLLLLLLLLLLLLLLLLL the time.

When Clem isn't sleeping she's usually MOANING about something, or telling me that I'm ANNOYING her, or tormenting Clive the fish by STARING at him, or flicking her tail against his tank.

But Clem is SUPER SMART so when she decides to be HELPFUL it's GREAT!

But sometimes she STILL makes fun of me and plays tricks on me, even when she's helping. Like the time I got stuck inside a wellington boot. I couldn't see because I got stuck HEAD FIRST but I knew she was there because I could hear her laughing.

So that's when I said, "CLEM! HELP!!"

Clem DIDN'T help. But I knew what would work. So I said, "Come on, Clem! I know you're there. I can SMELL YOU!" And that's when Clem got very annoyed.

She says that cats are much cleaner than dogs (so what?) and washes herself at least fifteen times a day! What a waste of time! Anyway, that's when Clem came up with an idea to get me out of the boot, and it was to PUSH ME DOWN THE STAIRS.

When I landed at the bottom I was FURIOUS and I was JUST about to bark at her when I realised that I wasn't stuck in the boot any more.

"Told you it would work!" said Clem, grinning widely.

I think Clem probably ENJOYED pushing me down the stairs but at least it got me out of the boot. I'd been stuck in there for over an HOUR!

So anyway, I think I know why Clem is a bit mean and she moans a lot and why she can be VERY unhelpful. It's because she's worried Maddy loves me more than her.

We both

Maddy because she is eight and she is

AWESOME.

But Clem gets a bit jealous sometimes because she used to have Maddy all to herself before me and Clive came along.

Maddy likes it when me and Clem are friends and so do I because a CAT BRAIN and a PUG BRAIN work very well together.

So I really, really, REALLY hope Clem decides to help me with my latest BIG IDEA because if it works it's going to make Maddy SO PROUD of me that she'll probably give us ONE HUNDRED belly rubs. And I LOVE belly rubs! And so does CLEM!

Chapter 2

I licked Maddy goodbye when she left for school and then I got started on my BEST IDEA EVER.

I was going to make a CAKE and send it to this brilliant TV show where everyone makes cakes in a big tent! But when I told Clem she said, “That’s a terrible idea. You’ll just make a MESS.” So that’s when I decided to show Clem just how BRILLIANT my idea was by making the YUMMIEST CAKE EVER.

I grabbed a notepad and pen and began drawing

up some plans. But then I remembered I don't like making plans. They're TOO DIFFICULT and TOO BORING and they make my pug brain feel like scrambled eggs.

So I decided just to start making the cake RIGHT AWAY because that would be more fun.

I KNEW I looked like a PROFESSIONAL BAKER in my apron and a fancy chef's hat that I'd made out of kitchen towel.

Clem rolled her eyes and said, "You look ridiculous, Pugly. PLEASE stop."

I was getting a bit annoyed with Clem. I'd hardly even started and she was being

UNHELPFUL

already. I tried to ignore her but she kept saying stuff like, "That mixture is a weird colour," and, "You're dropping egg shells in it," and, "I bet it tastes like feet," and that made me a little bit cross and VERY clumsy.

That's when I accidently dropped the eggs and slipped in all the yellow mess. And the flour went

Clem rolled her eyes at me and yawned. She didn't even TRY to help me clear up so I just licked the floor clean by myself.

Then I decided to ignore her and to STAY POSITIVE and keep making the cake. So I rushed around sprinkling sugar, cracking more eggs and pouring milk. Almost ALL of it went in the bowl, so that was good.

I eventually looked over at Clem. She was pretending to sleep but I noticed that she had one eye open a tiny bit. I KNEW that she was watching me so I did loads of fancy stuff to impress her like sieving the flour from REALLY high up and using FOUR WHISKS at the same time to give it all a final mix.

But then Clem jumped up on to the counter and narrowed her cat eyes at me. "You do know that your cake is NOT ACTUALLY going to win the competition, don't you?"

"Poor Clem," I said and patted her little cat head. "Maybe you need a nap."

I pointed at the cake tins I'd stacked on top of each other.

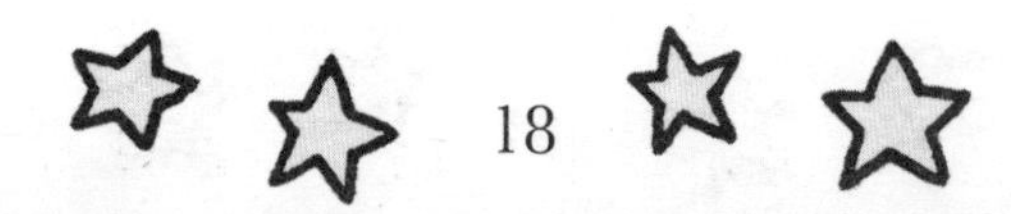

"I'm going to make a cake with TEN layers. Of COURSE it will win and Maddy will be so proud that she'll cuddle me FOR EVER! I hope she still has time to give you a little cuddle every now and then." I gave her my best wide-eyed innocent look.

Clem GLARED at me. Her tail began to flick really fast from side to side. Now I knew she was really annoyed but then she said sweetly, "You're right, Pugly. Maybe I SHOULD help."

"That would be BRILLIANT!" I said. I was really pleased that Clem wanted to help because I needed her to turn on the oven. My paws are too clumpy for fiddly knobs. She might even phone the TV people to get them to come and collect the cake!

I was SO EXCITED that I took my apron off and started running around the table because I LOVE running round and round the table when I'm happy. It is

THE BEST

THING TO DO

IN THE WORLD!

But THAT'S when I spotted HIM out of the corner of my eye. The Evil Squirrel was BACK. And he was sitting on MY fence. And I just KNEW that he was here to ruin my life and stop me winning the baking competition!

Chapter 3

"GET OUT OF HERE!" I barked over and over, and squished my face up against the window as MUCH as I could to try to scare the Evil Squirrel away.

But he just sat there on the fence STARING at me with his evil squirrel eyes. I got so angry that the Evil Squirrel wouldn't GET OFF MY FENCE that I suppose I got a BIT upset.

OK, fine. I went completely BERSERK.

I began barking and jumping up and down. Then I threw myself against the window. And the chair. And then the table. (I like throwing myself against things when I'm annoyed at the Evil Squirrel.) But then there was an almighty CLATTER and the cake-tin tower came crashing down to the ground all around me.

Oops!

"Congratulations," said Clem. "You've managed to bash up every single cake tin. Maybe NOW Maddy will see sense and make you live on a farm, with the other pigs."

I could feel myself getting even angrier. Clem's ALWAYS saying that I don't really look like a dog (because of my squashed face and curly tail) and that I'm probably really a pig. I keep telling her that I'm NOT a pig and that I'm a PUG and that ALL PUGS have faces and tails like mine. And that we are all

But she doesn't listen.

"It's not MY fault the cake tins are bashed up!" I huffed. "It was HIM!" I pointed at the fence but the Evil Squirrel was gone. The crashing noise must have scared him away.

"Who, Pugly? Who?" asked Clem, looking even more bored than usual.

"The Evil Squirrel, of course! He's ALWAYS spying on me. Every time I come up with a FANTASTIC IDEA, there he is on the fence!

Lurking.

Watching.

Waiting.

He must be stopped!"

"Oh, Pugly. What an imagination you have!" said Clem with a tinkling laugh. "There is NO Evil Squirrel out to get you. It must be all that weird food you eat."

"It's not weird food and

I yelled.

"Well, I don't see any squirrel," said Clem. "I just see YOU causing CHAOS as usual. I'm going for my mid-morning nap while you clear up this mess.

"Wait! I thought you were going to help me?"

Clem stopped suddenly, and then she turned and smiled at me.

"Oh. Yes. Of course. And I have an idea, actually. I saw it in one of Maddy's mum's new cookbooks."

So Clem jumped up and began reading the cookbook, but she wouldn't let me see, so I just had to sit and wait while she read and said things like "Ooooooh!" and "Magnificent!" and "Well, that's just

INSPIRED!"

and then she snapped the book shut.

"OUCH!"

I yelped. "My PAW!"

"Oh, dear. I'm dreadfully sorry," said Clem (even though she didn't look very sorry at ALL). "The recipe says that you need to add the following ingredients to your cake mix. As well as some tuna you need smelly Cheddar cheese and day-old spaghetti."

"What?" I said. Sometimes Clem's voice is a bit yowly and I don't always understand what she's saying.

Clem came really close to me and opened her cat-eyes WIDE. Her tail was flicking like mad. I began to feel a bit scared.

She explained that if I was SERIOUS about entering my cake into the TV baking competition in the big tent then I'd have to WOW the judges and do something

TOTALLY

UNIQUE.

"You have to make people GASP, Pugly," she said. And she was right.

"Maybe we should add even MORE ingredients?" I said. "We need to make a cake unlike ANY cake ANYONE has ever seen before!"

And that's when Clem's tail started flicking LOADS. "Onions," she said. "We must add onions." And again, she was right.

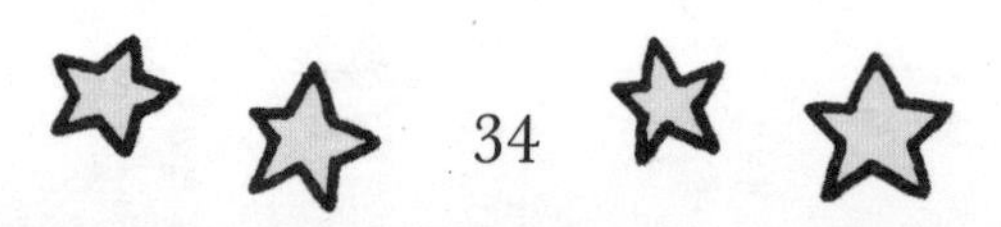

In the end, I got SO excited that I decided to add LOADS of leftover stuff that was in the fridge. Clem said that was a GREAT idea and then she called my cake a

"FUSION CAKE"

and

I LOVED

THAT

NAME!

Clem said she'd help by watching. She said even the best and most FAMOUS chefs on TV always have people standing around watching them cook, and talking to them. Then she curled up on the counter and went to sleep.

And that's when I heard the knocking. It didn't sound loud enough to be coming from the front door.

CLANK.
CLANK.
CLANK.

“Where is that noise coming from?” I said, looking around, and that’s when I spotted Clive. He’d picked up one of the pebbles from the bottom of his fish tank and was banging it against the glass.

"You're AWAKE!" I cried.

I love Clive, but he sleeps LOADS because he's a really old fish and he even has a bit of a beard. I was REALLY pleased to see him, because he's the BEST, but he was being a bit weird this morning. He was STARING at me, waving his fins around, and banging the stone against the glass again.

But then Clem woke up. She yawned, and wrapped herself silkily around Clive's tank. She looked at him and smiled, and the clanking stopped.

"That's better!" she purred. "Now, you must be quiet, Clive, while Pugly finishes his FUSION CAKE. I have to pop out for a minute."

And then she uncurled herself from Clive's tank and slipped out of the cat flap.

As soon as Clem was gone the CLANKING started again.

I clambered up on to the counter to see Clive. His little fish face was pressed RIGHT up against the glass. He looked worried.

“What is it, Clive?” I asked. “Is something the matter?”

Clive nodded LOADS and began blowing masses of bubbles at me.

“I’m sorry, Clive,” I said. “You know I can’t speak fish-bubble.”

He looked really worried again.

But then I had a

BRILLIANT

IDEA.

“Let’s play charades!” I said. “You can ACT OUT whatever it is you’re trying to tell me!”

Clive nodded eagerly. He pointed to his eyes and then pointed to my eyes.

“Yes, Clive, I’m watching!” I yelled. I was excited. I LOVED playing charades with Clive.

Clive began picking up loads of little stones and piling them on top of each other, in layers, like he was pretending to make a pie or a cake or something. Then he used his little fin to cut himself a slice of the stone cake and pretended to eat it.

But then all of a sudden, Clive's eyes went WIDE and he clutched his throat with both fins and began flopping all over the tank until eventually he fell down. Dead.

“NOOOOOOOOOOOOOOO!

CLIVE!

DON’T DIE!

CLIVE!”

I banged frantically on the glass with my paws. But he just lay there on the bottom of the tank, eyes closed and completely still.

I couldn’t believe it. Clive was DEAD! My BEST FRIEND WAS DEAD!

But then a MIRACLE happened! Clive sat up and opened his eyes. Clive was

ALIIIIIIIIIIIIIVE!

He was alive, but he looked very cross. He had his fins crossed and he was shaking his head at me and blowing bubbles out of the side of his mouth. I had no idea why. But I didn't care. He was alive! Clive was alive!

Then Clive did the eye thing again to make sure I was watching. Then he used the little stones to make a face. And the face was CLEM'S face! Then he started to write stone-words beneath the stone-picture of Clem. I didn't know what the words meant, but they looked like this:

CLEM HAS
TRICKED
YOU!

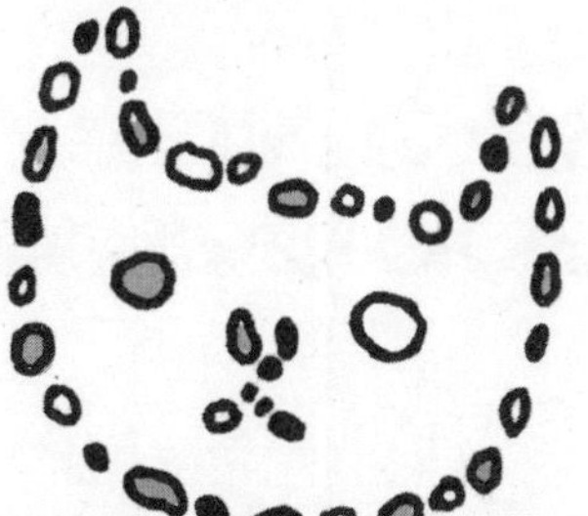

Chapter 5

"Hello, Clive," came an unexpected voice.

I got such a fright I sneezed three times in a row, all over Clive's fish tank.

"Stop sneaking up like that!" I yelled at Clem. "You're like a cat ninja!"

Clem had a weird look in her eyes. "Where's Clive gone?" she demanded.

"He's in there, of course," I said, pointing to the tank.

"I can't see him," said Clem angrily. "You've covered the glass in

PUG-SNEEZE!"

“Oh, sorry,” I said, wiping the glass clean with my paws. “He was just writing something interesting on the floor of his tank.”

Clem's eyes narrowed into tiny slits.

"I can't read it, of course. But you can read it for me!" I wagged my tail so hard at Clem that my bottom did a little salsa dance.

"How interesting!" she said, moving away from my wagging bottom. "Of COURSE I'll read you Clive's little message."

I finished cleaning the glass so that we could see Clive again and the stone words. But they had

"Clive!" I called. He appeared from behind some weeds, looking even more worried than before. "What happened to the words, buddy?" I asked.

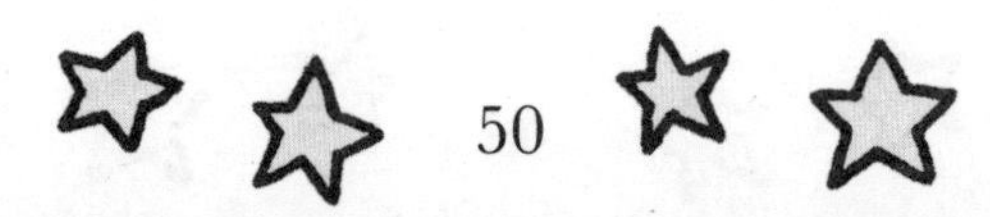

Clive looked scared.

"Yes, CLIVE," said Clem, sweetly. "What happened to them, BUDDY?"

Clive gulped and blew out a few tiny bubbles.

"What's he saying, Clem?" I asked. "Can you speak fish-bubble?"

"He's saying that your cake is going to be DELICIOUS!" said Clem, pushing her face up to the glass. "Isn't that right, Clive?"

I looked at Clive. He nodded slowly, and then winked at me when Clem looked away. I winked back. How cute! A wink must mean

I LOVE YOU

in fishy!

While the cake was baking I decided to call EVERYONE to tell them that I was going to be on TV and maybe even the news because I was the first dog EVER to bake a cake.

But Clem said that I should wait and show my MASTERPIECE to Maddy first, before I was taken off to be on TV and my cake was shown to the Queen and then put in a cake museum.

Clem said that I should take the FIRST BITE so Maddy could see how SPECIAL it was, and I agreed. I couldn't WAIT for Maddy to get home and be proud of me!

"Have you decided how you're going to DECORATE your cake once it's baked?" said Clem. Her tail was flicking wildly again. "Because I found a bag of EXTRA SPECIAL nuts in the cupboard. They're called PISTACHIO nuts and they're very EXPENSIVE and LUXURIOUS and Maddy's mum has been keeping them for a special occasion, just like this one."

"I don't know," I said. "Aren't nuts a bit boring?"

Clem smiled. "Not THESE ones," she said, holding out her paw.

I couldn't believe it. The nuts were bright GREEN!

"They're PERFECT!" I cried, spinning round and round. "I'm going to sprinkle them ALL OVER my cake. I mean, who WOULDN'T love a green cake?!

YUM!"

I got so excited that I knocked over the flour again. "Oops! Maybe I should clear up while the cake is baking," I suggested. The kitchen was looking a bit messy.

"Oh, don't you worry your little puggy head about that," said Clem. "I'll do it for you. You've worked SO hard today, Pugly. Why don't you go upstairs and have a little rest and leave EVERYTHING to me."

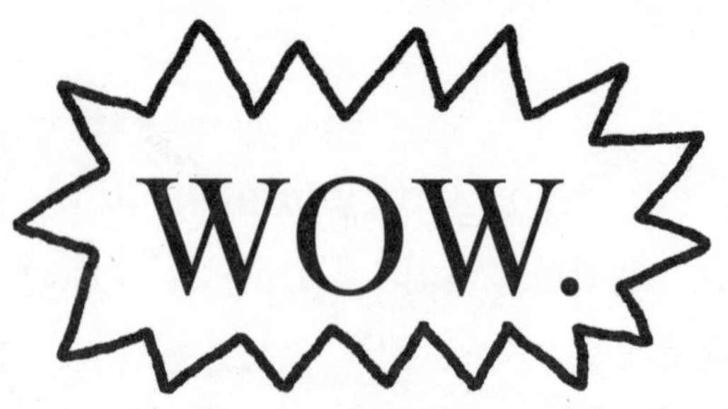

Clem was being so NICE suddenly. That sounded

WONDERFUL!

I mean, I WAS quite tired after all the mixing. Plus I needed to go through ALL of the drawers and cupboards upstairs until I found Maddy's dad's best bow tie for when I went on TV.

After my nap I felt FABULOUS. I'd had THE BEST dream ever. I'd dreamed that Maddy came home and tasted my cake and she loved it SO much that she bought me a hat that said BEST PET EVER on it and I wore it to the park and the cinema and when I had tea with the Queen (because I was famous, and that's what famous people do).

"CLEMMMMMMM!" I shouted down the stairs. "Do you think I should wear a HAT as well as a BOW TIE when I'm on the TV later?"

But Clem didn't answer.

I tried on all the hats I could find, but I didn't really like any of them (well, maybe the big flowery one but I couldn't really see when I had it on) so I decided just to wear the bow tie.

I looked in the mirror.

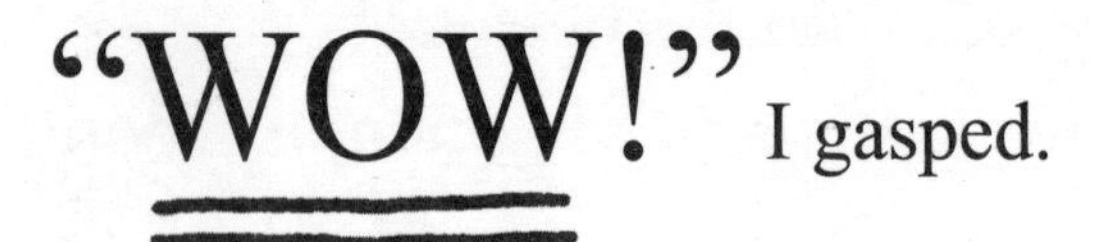

"CLEM! Come and look at me. I look

"CLEM?"

I thought it was weird that Clem hadn't replied or come upstairs to help me with the hats, so I went down to the kitchen to find her.

I gasped when I saw the mess in the kitchen. It looked even WORSE than when I'd gone up for a nap. The place was TRASHED!

And then I smelled the smell.

IT.

WAS.

DISGUSTING.

"EEEEUUUURRRGHHH!" I said. "Was that YOU, Clive?"

Clive had clearly PARPED a very bad fishy parp. I jumped up on the counter and reached up to see Clive. He might be able to tell me what had HAPPENED to the kitchen while I'd been sleeping. But Clive wasn't in his tank. He was GONE!

"CLEMMMMMMM!" I screamed. "Where ARE you? Someone's FISHNAPPED Clive!"

But Clem was nowhere to be seen.

That's when I remembered my cake.

What if someone had taken that, too?

I jumped down and ran over to the oven. Phew! The cake was still in there.

I put on my oven gloves and took the cake out and placed it on the counter.

That's when I realised where the smell was coming from. Something had gone HORRIBLY wrong. My cake STANK!

I tried to stay calm.

"Don't panic, Pugly," I told myself.

"You'll think of something."

THAT'S when my pug brain PINGED into action again and I realised what was REALLY going on. I'd figured out WHY the cake looked and smelled AWFUL. Of COURSE! I couldn't BELIEVE IT! I'd been such a FOOL!

I HADN'T ADDED THE PISTACHIO NUTS YET!

I quickly put the cake back in the oven and looked around the kitchen for the pistachios. They would fix

EVERYTHING!

I'd sprinkle them all over the cake, the smell would disappear, and then Clem would come back from wherever she'd gone, help me find Clive and then we'd all tidy up this mess before Maddy got home. But I couldn't find the pistachio nuts ANYWHERE.

And then I spotted him.

The Evil Squirrel.

He was sitting on the fence, munching.

"GET LOST!" I barked through the glass. "I don't have TIME for you just now."

I froze. Hang on! What WAS that he was munching? I pushed my face RIGHT up against the glass. He was holding something in his evil little paws … something GREEN!

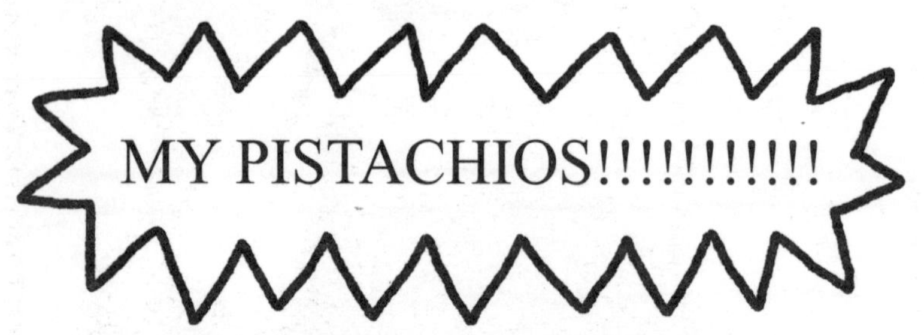

I went absolutely BERSERK! I had NO IDEA how the Evil Squirrel had got his hands on MY pistachio nuts. How did he get in here?

"The CAT FLAP!" I barked through the glass. "THAT'S how you got in here. THIEF! And just LOOK at the mess you've made!"

Then I gasped. “CLIVE! You FISHNAPPED him, didn’t you? Where are you hiding him? WHERE? You are

The Evil Squirrel just stared at me and kept munching. He seemed to be smiling a bit too.

I had to get out. I had to rescue Clive AND the rest of my pistachio nuts before the Evil Squirrel ruined EVERYTHING!

I looked at the cat flap. I was pretty sure I could fit through. Yes, no problem.

Chapter 8

Well, there was ONE problem. Maddy's mum had put a little wooden "doggy gate" in front of it to stop me trying to get outside by myself. This is VERY unfair because Clem is allowed out whenever she wants! She can jump over the little gate no problem at all, but my pug legs are too small and stumpy.

That's when I realised that what I needed was a TRAMPOLINE!

I raced around the house but I couldn't find one ANYWHERE. (Which was a bit weird. I mean, what kind of house doesn't have a trampoline?)

But then my pug brain went WILD and I had one of my

BEST IDEAS EVER!

I'd make my OWN trampoline!

I pulled ALL the cushions off the sofa and made a cushion tower so that I could bounce over the doggy gate. But I kept falling over before I could reach the top because the cushions were SO ANNOYING and wouldn't stay in place.

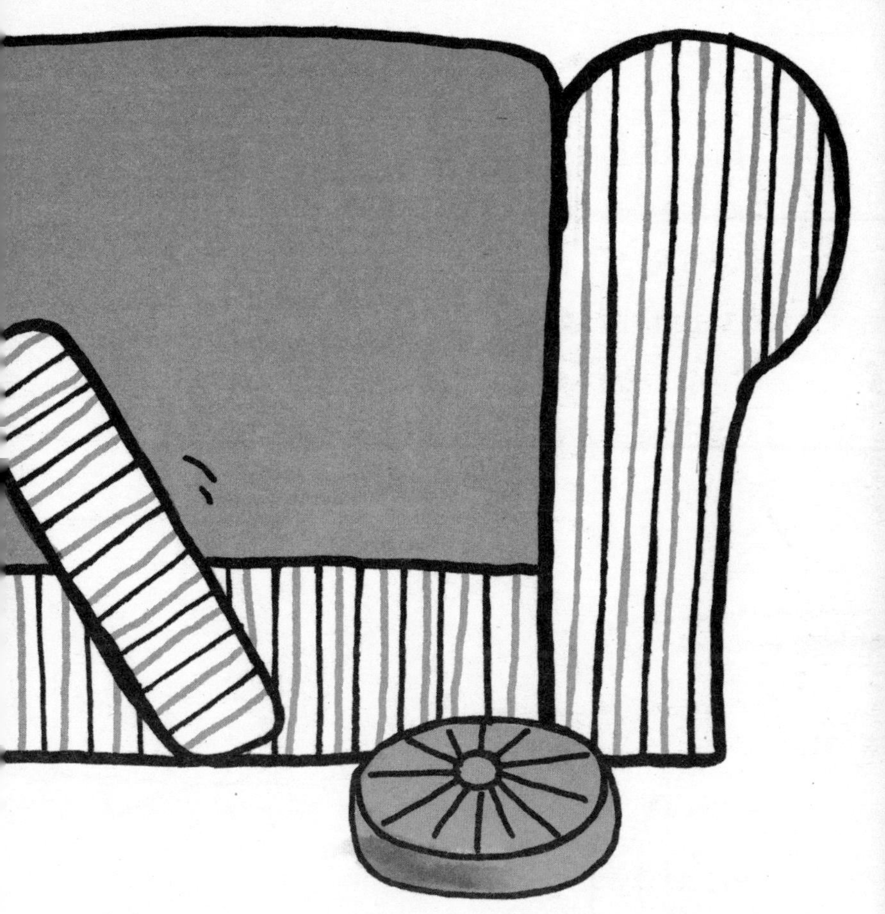

I got SO MAD at the cushions that I started stomping all over them and shaking them around in my mouth, and throwing myself ALL OVER the place because my plan wasn't working, and then all of a sudden I heard a CRASH.

It took me a minute to realise what had happened. I'd had such a big PUG TANTRUM that I'd gone CRASHING through the doggy gate! I was FREE!

I was so excited that I ran as fast as I could towards the cat flap and leaped through it the way Clem did.

And that's when I got stuck.

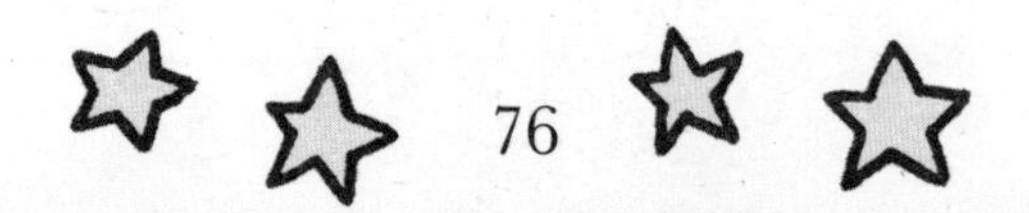

Chapter 9

I looked up at the Evil Squirrel. He was still staring and munching (evilly).

"THIS IS ALL YOUR FAULT!" I barked at him.

Just then a large dog with very long hair wandered up to our back fence and the Evil Squirrel disappeared.

"Hey man," said Chester. "How you doing?"

I was pleased to see Chester because he could save me. But he did like to talk quite a lot.

"Dude!" he said. "Have you heard the big news? I'm sure you have. You've probably seen me on the front of the YEAH VEG! dog food in the local health-food shop, right?"

I had no idea what Chester was talking about.

Also, I'd like to point out that Chester didn't even seem to NOTICE that I was trapped. He was too busy talking and talking and TALKING!

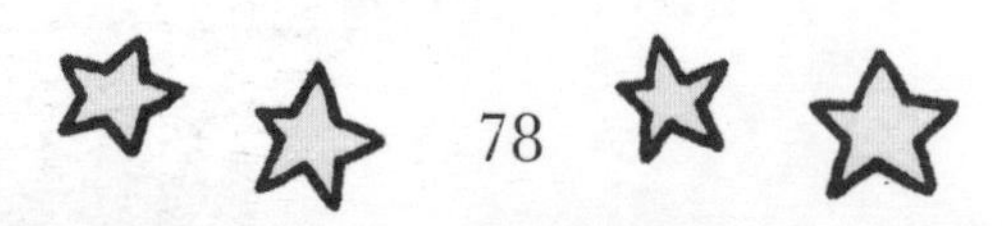

"I'm a full-time model for YEAH VEG! now, Pugs," he was saying. "It's pretty awesome. My owner, Leo, makes all the food himself in our kitchen. It's all real good stuff, man. Full of yummy veggies!"

"Chester, listen to me," I said. But it was no use, he wouldn't stop yapping.

"I gotta work out in the park at least four times a day to keep in shape," he continued as he showed me his legs.

"I do yoga mostly.

Sometimes I meditate.

Being a model can be stressful. I need a lot of ‘me time’ before a photoshoot, man.”

I gave up. Chester wasn’t listening to me at

ALL.

"And I'm not ashamed to say I get my hair done every Saturday. A dog's gotta look nice for the ladies, am I right?!

"Speaking of ladies, is Clem around? That is one cool cat. I wonder if she likes my new 'do?" Chester said, flicking his long hair around.

I started barking frantically. "I don't know where Clem is but I REALLY need to find her, Chester! The Evil Squirrel's fishnapped Clive and stolen the pistachio nuts and ruined the kitchen and I'm supposed to be on TV tonight with my cake!"

"WHOA! Dude! That sounds like heavy stuff. You need to CHILLAX. Let me help you."

And then Chester jumped over the fence and wandered towards me. FINALLY he was going to stop talking and

GET ME OUT!

But he didn't.

Chester sat down and began crossing his legs in all sorts of weird ways. "You know, ever since we moved here from California, I've tried to set a good example to all the dogs in the village," he said. "They all come to me for advice, you know. They're like, 'WOW! Chester, you look amazing, man! What's your secret? I wanna be just like you! HIGH FIVE!' And I'm like, 'You gotta take care of yourselves, guys. Eat right, work out and aim high. Positive vibes, man.'"

Chester held my paws in his and then closed his eyes. I thought he was going to pull me out. He didn't.

"I guess you could call me a role model," he said. "It's like I always say, not everyone can be as awesome as me, but it can't hurt to try!"

Then Chester EVENTUALLY stopped talking and starting HUMMING. I think he was MEDITATING (whatever that is) and he did it for a really, really, REALLY long time.

That's when I realised that I needed a wee! But I was STUCK! I started to panic.

"Chester!"

But Chester was humming so loudly he couldn't even hear me.

Oh no. Oh no. Oh no. My FRONT half was outside. But my BOTTOM half (including my actual bottom) was still inside the kitchen. I HAD to get out. I wiggled as hard as I could and kicked my little legs like I do when I'm swimming.

"WHAT are you two doing?" came an angry voice from behind Chester.

I got SUCH a fright I started weeing.

It was Clem. I stared at her as I continued to wee on the kitchen floor.

"And just HOW am I supposed to get back inside NOW?" Clem asked.

At first I wondered why Clem wasn't going MAD about me weeing on the kitchen floor (VERY close to her food bowl) but then I realised that she couldn't see my bottom half through the door. So I could EASILY pretend that I wasn't weeing.

"Oh, hey Clem!" said Chester as he jumped up and began swishing his hair all over the place.

Clem ignored Chester completely and just stared at me without blinking. She was WAY too close to my face.

"Get. Out. Now," she said.

"I can't! I'M STUCK!"

"Well, you CAN'T be stuck because it's MY cat flap and MY bed is in there and I have to take a nap immediately. I've just had a large lunch," she said, licking her whiskers.

"Dudes, what's that smell?" said Chester. "Something smells fishy. Not cool."

Clem's tail began flicking again.

It took me a minute to realise that Chester was talking about the cake. It really DID smell bad.

"Thank goodness I brought this with me,

man," said Chester as he began spraying himself with perfume. "That bogus smell is getting in my hair."

Clem narrowed her eyes at me.

"We'll just have to think of something to get you out of there," she said.

I sighed with relief. Thank GOODNESS Clem was here! Now maybe I could get her to help me fix the gate and clean up the wee and everything would be OK again. I wouldn't get told off and I would still be Maddy's favourite pet. Hooray!

"Has your lovely cake finished baking?" said Clem, over-nicely.

I couldn't BELIEVE I'd forgotten to tell Clem everything that had happened. It was because I was weeing. I always forget what's going on when I wee. So I concentrated really hard (because I was still doing a wee) and told Clem EVERYTHING. I told her all about the hats that didn't suit me, and the mess in the kitchen, and the fishnapping, and the smelly cake that I couldn't fix because of the stolen pistachio nuts, and the Evil Squirrel.

By the time I'd finished my story I'd also stopped weeing.

"We need to find Clive RIGHT AWAY!" I said. "The Evil Squirrel has taken him!"

But Clem didn't look very upset about ANY of it. She didn't even BLINK.

"OK. Close your eyes," she said. "This is going to hurt."

"WHAT?!"

And then Clem stuck one of her kitty claws RIGHT into my ear!

"OOOOOOOOOOOOOOWWWW! That HURT! WHAT are you DOING?"

"I'm trying to unstick you, you silly dog!"

"How is jabbing your CLAW into my ear going to help?!"

"Well. I thought it might make you GET BACK INSIDE THE HOUSE WHERE YOU BELONG!"

"Clem, you're one tough señorita!" said Chester. "That's cool. I like it."

"Well I DON'T!" I yelled. "And I'm STILL stuck!"

"Calm down, Pugly. Here, this might help you chillax," said Chester. And then he sprayed perfume IN MY FACE. The sticky perfume went right up my nose and made me do loads of pug sneezes one after the other. I could hear Clem laughing at me.

But then I felt a BIG sneeze coming. The kind of sneeze where you just KNOW you better shut your eyes tight or your eyeballs are going to pop out.

"AAAAACCCCHHHOOOOOOO!"

I sneezed so hard that I sent myself shooting back into the house. I was FREE!

"At LAST!" yelled Clem. "Get out of my way, Pugly. I'm coming in!"

THAT'S when I remembered that I was sitting in a puddle of my own wee (a BIG puddle).

Uh OH!

Clem's face was pure horror as she flew through the cat flap and realised what was about to happen.

"NOOOOOOOOOOOO!" she screeched as she tried to change direction in mid-air.

But it didn't work. She landed right in my piddle-puddle!

Once Clem had hissed at me and run away, I sat in the piddle-puddle for a while trying to think of a BRILLIANT PLAN.

The kitchen was still a mess and now there was wee all over the floor. The doggy gate was broken, my pistachio nuts were gone, Clive was missing and my cake really did smell fishy! I froze as the penny dropped.

"SOMEONE'S PUT CLIVE IN THE CAKE!"

I rushed to the oven and took the cake out again. It still smelled DISGUSTING.

"CLIVE!" I screamed at the cake. "Are you in there? I'm SO SORRY. Who did this to you? Was it the Evil Squirrel?"

I looked up at Clive's tank. He was BACK!

"CLIVE! I thought the Evil Squirrel had fishnapped you and baked you in my cake!"

Clive looked confused. He shook his head and pointed to the weeds in his tank. Then he put his fins under his head, closed his eyes and tilted his head like he was sleeping.

That's when I realised that Clive HADN'T been fishnapped. He'd just been sleeping in his weeds.

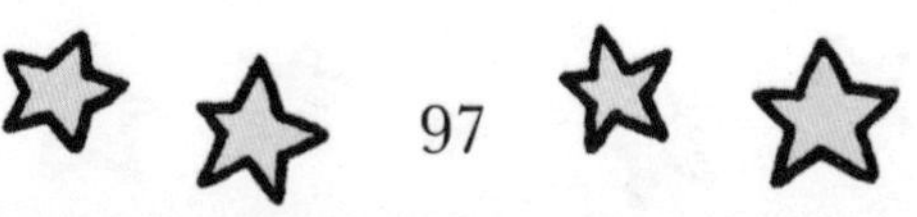

"My cake smells disgusting. It's RUINED!" I cried. "Someone must've put something yucky in it. I bet it was the Evil Squirrel!"

Clive started flicking his tail and narrowing his eyes like Clem does.

"HA! That's brilliant, Clive. You look just like Clem when you do that," I said.

Clive's eyes went wide and he began nodding furiously.

And then all of a sudden I realised what Clive had been trying to tell me earlier.

"Oh, PAWS!" I cried. "It was CLEM, wasn't it? She

TRICKED

ME!

I should have KNOWN that cheese and tuna and spaghetti and ONIONS don't belong in a CAKE. She WANTED my cake to be a disaster, didn't she?"

Clive nodded.

"Maddy is going to KILL YOU!" said Clem, appearing from nowhere. "The kitchen is a MESS, you've smashed the doggy gate AND you've made the MOST DISGUSTING CAKE IN THE WORLD!"

Before I could answer, I heard a key turn in the lock. I gasped and stared at Clem.

"This is all your fault, Clem. What if Maddy tries to eat the cake and gets really ill? You have to help me fix this. It's an EMERGENCY."

Clem looked a bit worried then and quick as a flash, she leaped up and knocked Clive's fish tank off the counter. The water went ALL OVER the cake and it crumbled and dissolved into a horrible puddle on the kitchen floor.

"CLIIIIIIIIIIIIIIVE!" I screamed as I watched him fall through the air. I rushed to catch him. But then he did a TRIPLE SOMERSAULT and landed right in the water jug with a loud PLOP!

IT.

WAS.

AMAZING!

I looked back at Clem. Her eyes darted towards the cat flap. I knew EXACTLY what she was thinking. She was going to try to escape so that I would have to take the blame for the tank and all the mess. I knew what I had to do. I looked up at Clive and he winked at me.

"HA!" I cried as I launched myself at the cat flap. "No way will I let you escape. You'll have to stay and get the blame for what you've done!" Before Clem realised what was happening I had got myself totally stuck. Again.

I couldn't see what was happening, of course, because pugs don't have eyes in their bottoms, but Maddy must have walked in at that moment because I heard Clem start making pathetic whimpering sounds.

"CLEMENTINE!" cried Maddy. "What have you

DONE?!"

I barked as loudly as I could and waggled my curly tail to let Maddy know where I was. You know, just in case she didn't notice my bottom hanging out of the cat flap.

"Pugly! Are you OK? Oh my goodness!"

It took Maddy ages to unscrew the cat flap and get me out. When I was back on the other side I got

Maddy wasn't mad at me at ALL. But she WAS mad at Clem because she knew that it had been her who knocked over Clive's fish tank because Maddy is FOREVER telling Clem to stay away from the tank.

Clem didn't get ANY cuddles OR belly rubs!

Later that night when we were watching TV, Clem came skulking into the room and sat in the corner with her back to us, just staring at the wall, sulking.

Maddy started giggling when she saw her. “Come here, naughty little Clemmy,” she said. And Clem RACED over and jumped up next to me on Maddy’s knee and began purring like mad while we all watched *The Great British Bake Off*.

The Evil Squirrel

Hi. My name's Josh. How are you? I'm great. I just ate forty-seven nuts. They were brilliant! Best nuts I've ever had. Extra nutty. The nice cat gave them to me. I think her name's Clementine. She's lovely. Not like that pug. He's mean. He always barks at me. And chases me away. This time I wasn't even doing anything. I was just WATCHING, for nuts' sake. There's no law against it. I don't understand why he hates me so much. I mean, what did I ever do to him?!